ORBIT WIPEOUT!

Look for these

titles, coming soon:

#3
MONDO MELTDOWN

#4
INTO THE ZONK ZONE!

And don't miss

#1
SPACE BINGO

ORBIT WIPEOUT!
by Tony Abbott

Illustrated by Kim Mulkey

A SKYLARK BOOK
NEW YORK·TORONTO·LONDON·SYDNEY·AUCKLAND

RL 4, 007–010

ORBIT WIPEOUT!
A Skylark Book / March 1996

Skylark Books is a registered trademark of Bantam Books, a division of
Bantam Doubleday Dell Publishing Group, Inc. Registered in U.S. Patent and
Trademark Office and elsewhere.

Time Surfers is a series by
Bantam Doubleday Dell Books for Young Readers,
a division of Bantam Doubleday Dell Publishing Group, Inc.

Cover art by Frank Morris
Interior illustrations by Kim Mulkey
Cover and interior design by Beverly Leung

ISBN 0-553-48304-8

Published simultaneously in the United States and Canada.

Bantam Books are published by Bantam Books, a division of Bantam Doubleday
Dell Publishing Group, Inc. Its trademark, consisting of the words "Bantam
Books" and the portrayal of a rooster, is Registered in U.S. Patent and
Trademark Office and in other countries. Marca Registrada. Bantam Books,
1540 Broadway, New York, New York 10036.

PRINTED IN THE UNITED STATES OF AMERICA

10   9   8   7   6   5   4   3   2   1

OPM

For Irene and Dolor,
the best parents-in-law
a writer could ever hope to have

ORBIT WIPEOUT!

CHAPTER
1

"There is no such thing as time travel!" said the deep voice. "It only happens in stories or on television or in comic books!"

Ned Banks was sitting at his new desk in his new school, listening to his new teacher and trying hard not to scream.

". . . it is absolutely impossible . . ."

Ned watched as Mr. Smott walked back and forth in front of the class, squinting up at the ceiling as if he had notes written up there, and droning on and on. It was so boring it was almost painful.

But the worst part was that it was totally wrong!

Ned glanced over at the kids in the row next to him. They were all taking notes. They didn't know what Ned knew. No one in the whole world did.

Time travel *was* possible.

Ned was certain of it. In fact—he smiled to himself—he, Ned Banks, new kid in school, total nerd by day, was an official, intergalactic, planet-saving Time Surfer!

It had all started one night a couple of weeks earlier, when Ned had finished building a personal communicator so that he could call his friend Ernie Somers. Ernie lived a thousand miles away in Newton Falls, Ned's hometown.

". . . no one can change how time works . . ."

But that night something had gone wrong. The communicator had opened something called a timehole in Ned's closet, and two kids from the future had blasted in!

Roop Johnson and Suzi Naguchi were two silver-suited Time Surfers from the year

2099. They traveled through timeholes, surfing from one time to another and back again.

And they took Ned with them. Into time.

Into the future.

Ned tapped his back pocket. *Yes.* The communicator was there. He always carried it.

Mr. Smott walked over to the blackboard and began writing. "Time travel cannot happen in real life, because . . ."

Ned smiled to himself. *Wrong.*

In 2099, as it turned out, kids pretty much ruled the world. They did everything. Grownups did some stuff, of course. But the really major-cool things, like deep-space missions, zooming around in time, going to other planets in souped-up spaceships called surfies—that was total kid stuff in 2099.

Ned had become an official Time Surfer after he saved Earth from total destruction when a comet was heading straight for it.

Nobody in this century knew that, either.

Except Ernie. He and Ned were best friends. They told each other everything. Ernie was the only one who knew about the

Time Surfers. Ned knew he could trust Ernie. Completely.

Ned glanced up. Mr. Smott was still writing on the board. Something about time being a straight line.

Ned shook his head slightly. *Wrong, wrong, wrong!* It wasn't like that at all. Time looped all around. Forward and backward. Into the future and back to the past.

To the past . . .

Ned's mind drifted. Back to his old school. To his old classroom. To the thing with the cards . . .

It had happened back in Newton Falls Elementary, just as his class had been taking out their language books.

Ernie was showing Ned his cards. Not just any cards. His *Special Zero Series Deluxe Edition Ice Planet Commandos Zebra Force Legends of Zontar* cards.

Ned and Ernie collected Zontar comic books. That's where Ned had gotten the idea for the communicator. And when the cards came out, they collected those, too. Ernie had been the first one in their class to get a complete set. Thirty-six cards.

Those cards were amazing. The two most amazing ones in the collection were foil-embossed 3-D hologram-stamped cards. One showed an enormous Klenn warrior, one of the evil, bumpy-faced green alien creatures that were always attacking Earth.

But the prize of the collection, the best one, was the other foil-embossed 3-D hologram-stamped card. It showed Zontar himself, the awesome hero of Zebra Force, laughing as he prepared to deal earthshaking blows to wave upon wave of evil Klenn.

"Zontar is so cool! Can you imagine if he was real? He'd be huge!" Ernie had said. "And I love the stuff he says when he battles the Klenn."

Ned hulked up his shoulders, frowned, and lowered his voice. "Pee-yew! Is that a Klenn I smell? I'll have to hold my nose while I clobber him!"

Klenn were very smelly. They had these

gross slimy breathing tubes that hung over their shoulders. It was disgusting.

"Steng-o hodd!" said Ernie. That was Klenn for "Kill everyone!"

Zontar was like a huge space cowboy. He wore all kinds of armor. He was very tough, but he was always ready with some kind of joke as he crushed the evil aliens. Zontar was on cereal boxes and candy bars. He even had his own morning cartoon and video game as well as the comic book and cards.

"Awesome!" Ned gasped as Ernie fanned out the whole set of shiny new cards.

Ernie smiled. "At recess we'll read them all straight through. Let me just get them in order—"

Their teacher cleared her throat. Ned turned to his language book and looked up at her.

The room grew silent.

Ernie fiddled with his cards.

"Class," the teacher began, "today we'll start with—"

F-f-f-f-f-t-t-t-t-t-t-t-t-t-t!

Thirty-six *Legends of Zontar* cards suddenly blasted from Ernie's hands like lava from a volcano.

Cards were everywhere.

Some plinked against the fluorescent lights on the ceiling. Others skipped and fluttered across the room to the blackboard. One card got stuck between the teacher's glasses and her nose.

Ernie was everywhere, too, trying to catch every single card before it hit the floor.

Ned laughed. The kids laughed. Even the teacher laughed.

Ernie finally laughed, too, at recess. That's when he tapped the cards into a neat stack and handed them to Ned. "Keep them."

"What?" Ned gasped. "But it took you weeks to collect all those cards. It's the Deluxe Edition! Why?"

"I don't know. Because." Ernie shrugged. "Because we're best friends."

What he meant was, because Ned was moving away. A thousand miles away to a place called Lakewood. To Lakewood

School. To no friends. To Mr. Smott. To the droning and droning and droning.

"Another reason time travel can't work is . . ."

Ned snapped out of his daydream and slowly slipped the stack of Zontar cards he kept in his back pocket to his lap. The foil glinted under the overhead lights.

All he had to do was make it through class, go to gym, then—Ernie!

Yes! he thought. *In a few short hours Ernie will actually be here. For a whole week! Ernie's going to spend his school vacation with me!*

It was going to be great. Ned and Ernie, just like the old days. Reading Zontar comics. Flipping cards. Chomping snacks in front of the TV. Shooting hoops. Telling gross-out alien stories.

Ned looked down at the cards in his lap. Yeah, it was going to be tremendous, just the two of—

Wait. Something was different. The droning.

It wasn't there anymore.

Ned looked up from his cards. His nose brushed Mr. Smott's nose.

"Trading cards, Mr. Banks?" the teacher shouted. *"In* my *class?"*

Ned's mouth dropped open. He looked around. Everyone was staring at him.

"Uh—Mr. Smott—I—uh—" Ned glanced from his teacher to the stack of cards in his hands, then back again.

The class snickered as Mr. Smott grabbed the cards, stormed up the aisle, and slapped them down with a loud *smack* on his own desk.

* * *

Smack!

The next thing Ned knew, the bell had rung and he was outside, scrambling across the grass at full speed, trying to catch a very high, very fast fly ball.

A runner was zooming past first base.

"Run, Banks, run!" Coach Fensterman

yelled, throwing his cap down and stomping on it.

Suddenly—*kkkkkkrrrkkkkk!* The air crackled like lightning.

A breeze blew across the infield, kicking up a cloud of dust.

Over his shoulder, Ned could see the runner pumping on his way to third. He was going to score! The other team would win the game!

Then, out of the dust swirling around second base, a dark shape appeared and blazed toward the outfield.

Ned kept running back.

Kids were yelling. Dust was everywhere.

Ned reached up to grab the baseball. His feet left the ground as he leaped.

The cloud rolled completely over him.

Roarrrr! The sound of engines?

Ka-chung! The sound of metal?

A second later—*umph!*—Ned hit a metal floor. Hard.

He looked up to see two silver heads with large green eyes bending over him.

CHAPTER 2

"Aaaah!" screamed Ned, scrambling backward.

The two silver-headed, green-eyed creatures raised their hands, snapped their fingers, and waved.

Ned stopped. He looked. He blinked.

The snap wave! The official Time Surfer greeting!

Flink! Flink! Glowing green visors on the two silver heads flipped up at the same time. And two familiar faces smiled at him.

"Roop! Suzi! Hey, you guys scared me!"

"Sorry for the quick pickup, Ned," said

Suzi Naguchi, giving him a smile. "But we're on a mission and we need you."

Suzi had her short black hair tucked behind her ears. She tugged lightly on the control stick, and the odd-shaped purple ship flashed across the outfield, veered up over the bleachers, and went straight into the air.

"Yeah, and good thing we came along when we did, Nedbuddy," added Roop Johnson, pointing down at the field. "You just about got bageled down there!"

That was another thing about these two. Sometimes the things they said were . . . strange.

The little spaceship shot high over the school parking lot.

Ned remembered the first time he had seen the ship, stuck sideways in his closet the night he'd tried to call Ernie on his communicator.

Suzi had called it a hypermodal antigravity warp-class chronoprojection surfer, otherwise known as a surfie.

It was awesome and it was fast. It was

also standard kid equipment in 2099. Now, as the surfie banked around the gym, Ned noticed two extra bumps between the big fins on the back.

"Afterburners," said Roop. "For the hyperwarp capacitator, of course! Now this baby can really zoom!"

"And we were zooming in your zone," Suzi said, "when we caught an urgent message from Spider Base. We're going now to check it out!"

"So hold on, Neddo!" cried Roop. "We'll show you what this rig can do!"

"Wait!" Ned looked down at the ground from the surfie. The dust cloud spread across the field. "I can't! I mean, Ernie's coming later. He's spending the week with me! I've gotta get back!"

Roop turned and flashed a big smile at Ned. "Did you forget how we operate, Neddo? We'll get you back. At exactly the same time you left. No prob!"

Time travel was weird. If you got back at exactly the moment you left, everything was fine. No one even knew you'd been gone. But if you didn't—well, things got pretty scary!

"Can we at least make a stop?" asked Ned. "I need something from school."

Suzi shot a look at Roop. He wagged his head back and forth a couple of times, then nodded. "Really fast, Nedman. Then we blast!"

"Take a left at the flagpole," Ned instructed.

Zip-zip! The rear fins flipped in, the surfie got skinny, and—*whoom!*—it dived through the front doors into the main hall of Lakewood School.

"Oh, and by the way, Ned," said Suzi, pointing to Ned's glove, "nice catch."

Ned opened his glove. There, nestled snugly in the glove's pocket, was a baseball.

"Hey, I caught it! I actually caught it! Of course, with all the dust no one saw me," Ned moaned. "Just my luck. I make a terrific catch, and no one knows."

Voom! The surfie banked around the corner at the end of the hallway and shot straight up the stairs.

"So, Neddo," said Roop. "What do they call you now that you've saved Earth from becoming a major galactic pancake? Ned the Planet Saver? Or maybe something simple, like King Ned?"

Ned laughed. "Try Ned the Nerd. The newspapers said the big explosion was just some freaky weather thing. And I was so tired from all that time traveling that I fell asleep in class. Mr. Smott made this big frown and sent a note to my parents. Some hero. For saving the planet, I got grounded for a week."

"Grounded?" Roop winced. "Sounds bad. Is that like low-altitude surfing?"

"It's like *no*-altitude surfing. No TV, no nothing!"

Suzi gave Ned a pat on the back. "It must be tough being a Time Surfer back in your time."

Ned nodded. "Kind of like a superhero who protects his identity by being a dork."

The surfie slowed to cruising speed.

The halls of Lakewood School were deserted, and the afternoon sun shined through the windows in the classrooms as the surfie passed by.

"Not quite Spider Base," Ned said.

"They have lockers like these on display in a museum I went to once," Roop said.

"I believe it." Ned turned to Suzi. "My classroom is at the end. I just need a second to grab my stuff."

Suzi powered down the engines, guided the surfie around the corner, and parked it. She gave Ned a green visor to wear over his face. She and Roop put theirs on, too. "Powershades. Just in case. So no one recognizes us."

Ned slid on his green powershades and looked around. Everything was tinted green but was super-clear. No glare. "Cool. Too bad I don't have a silver suit. Then we could all look like aliens!"

Quietly he led the way into his classroom. Suzi closed the door behind them.

"Gotta get my cards—" Ned began to say. Then he froze.

Spread out across Mr. Smott's desk were his *Legends of Zontar* cards.

In order. From beginning to end. As if someone had been reading them.

"Mr. Smott!" gasped Ned. "He read my cards!"

A shiver ran down his spine as he pictured his teacher going over the cards. "Whoa! I can just see him frowning. And after what happened in class today, he's got to be looking for ways to get back at me!"

Ned quickly scooped up the cards.

Suzi went for the door. "Then we'd better blast! We sure don't want anyone to find us—"

Wham!

Too late. The door swung open.

And in stepped Mr. Smott.

CHAPTER 3

"*What's going on here?*" cried Mr. Smott. "Who are you, and what are you doing in my—"

"Time to go!" Ned screamed from behind his powershades. He shoved the cards into his pocket and whirled around, looking for a way to vanish.

"I think I hear my mom calling me," said Roop. He immediately jumped, dropped, and dived between Mr. Smott's legs and out into the hall.

Mr. Smott looked down. "Why, you— *alien!*"

"I'll take that as a compliment!" yelled Roop.

Suzi leaped up on a desk and catapulted over the teacher's head. "Gotta fly. Bye!" She was in the hall in a flash.

A second later—*rrrr!* Ned heard the surfie start up.

"Don't leave me here!" He tried to scoot around his teacher, but he tripped on a desk leg and fell onto an AV cart near the front of the room. It started to roll.

"Oh no you don't!" Mr. Smott shouted, lunging for Ned. "You can't escape me now!"

Errrr! The cart's front wheels caught Mr. Smott's foot as it skidded toward the door.

Ned tried to hold on, but the cart spun and smacked the wall with such force that he was thrown into the hallway feet first.

Mr. Smott rushed for the door and tried to grab Ned by the ankle. *Rrrrr!* The surfie flew around the corner and dipped just outside the classroom door.

"Jump in!" yelled Roop.

"Owww!" Ned crumpled into his seat as

the surfie blasted down the stairwell into the main hall. "Man! He almost had me!"

Ned struggled to sit upright as the surfie careened through the halls.

"We need a timehole, pronto!" shouted Roop.

"The refrigerator in the cafeteria?" asked Suzi.

"No!" said Ned, shuddering. "There might be turkey cubes left from lunch today. Those things can be pretty scary!"

"Then you'd better flip on your beamer and find us a way to the future!" Roop told him.

"One timehole coming up." Ned pulled his communicator from his back pocket. "Since you souped this up, Roop, I can find timeholes anywhere."

"I *loooove* to customize!" yelped Roop.

Ned pressed a small green button.

Diddle-iddle-eep! The box began to vibrate.

"Suzi, take a quick left, and—"

They screeched into a short corridor.

"—through those doors!"

The surfie knocked open a set of double doors and blasted into the school gym toward the stage at the far end.

The large room was empty. But not for long.

As soon as the surfie lifted toward the stage, the back doors of the gym swung open and Mr. Smott ran across the wooden floor.

"Hurry!" yelled Ned. The surfie dived for the heavy stage curtains swaying before them.

"I'm following you!" Mr. Smott screamed.

"Not likely!" said Roop, flipping a switch on the ship's main control panel. "Power down!"

Zip-zip! The surfie's tail fins pulled themselves in. The ship quivered once, slipped sideways between the curtains, and entered a timehole.

Ka-voom! Shimmering darkness surrounded them, and in an instant Lakewood School was miles away and years in the past.

"To the future!" shouted Suzi.

Ned gripped his flight seat. The force was incredible, pushing him deeper and deeper into the cushions.

Seconds later, when the purple surfie spun out of a timehole over Mega City, where Time Surfer headquarters was located, the year was 2099.

"Ah!" Suzi sighed. "Home sweet home."

Ned looked down on the vast city of spiral towers, blinking lights, and floating buildings. Dozens of other brightly colored flying ships soared and zoomed around them.

In the distance far below was the giant blue dome of Spider Base.

"And," Roop added, "dome sweet dome!"

"I still can't believe it," said Ned. "The future is so incredible, so big, so—different! Earth sure has changed in a hundred years."

Suzi turned from the controls and smiled. "Not everything's different, Ned. I was jacked into the Spider Base computer the other day and found out that your school is still around."

Ned shuddered. "Whoa!" he said. "Lakewood School? I wonder if I made it out alive." He paused. "Oh no!"

"What is it, Ned?" asked Suzi.

"I was just thinking. What if Mr. Smott is still there?"

"Maybe we'll do a flyby one of these days," said Roop. "You can check it out."

"No thanks!" said Ned. "I don't want to know that much!"

Weee-oop! Weee-oop! Zeep! Zeep!

An alarm sounded from the control console.

"Message from Spider Base," a voice intoned.

It was Buzzy, the surfie's talking onboard computer. "And I would say the message sounds urgent!" Buzzy liked to add little details of his own.

"Thanks, Buzz Boy," said Roop. "Screen on!"

The black screen in front of them brightened to blue, and a face appeared.

"Hi, Mom!" said Roop.

"Hi, honey." It was Commander Johnson,

Roop's mother. She was one of the top scientists at Spider Base. "Hello, Suzi. And welcome back to the future, Ned."

"Thanks," he said. "I can't wait to visit the base again."

Commander Johnson frowned. "I'm sorry, Ned. Not on this mission."

Mission. Ned loved the sound of that word.

"We received a signal from deep space," the commander said. "And our analysis shows that it came from Centaur One. Centaur was a tech station built during the shadow wars."

"The shadow wars?" said Ned.

"It's what we call the time before kids took over," Suzi explained.

"Yeah," said Roop. "There were some bad people fighting in deep space. Way bad."

The surfie soared through the center of a blinking orange O-shaped building floating above the city. The blinking lights spelled out *Mega City Donut Mall.*

"But since then, kids' rule is total," Suzi

added. Then she shot a glance at Commander Johnson's face on the screen. "Well, grown-ups do lots of stuff, too."

"Uh-huh," said Ned.

"Centaur was abandoned about thirty years ago," the commander went on. "This signal could be nothing more than a technical blip, a short circuit. Or it could be something else. Time Surfer Squad One, you should proceed immediately to Centaur and send a report."

"We're locked in and on our way," said Roop.

"Oh, and Roop?" the commander added.

"Yes, Mom?"

"Be home for supper." Commander Johnson gave them a quick snap wave, and the screen went dark.

"Whoa!" gasped Ned. "A mission in deep space! I still can't believe you do this kind of stuff. It's too cool to be real!"

Roop swiveled his seat so that he was facing a set of speed controls. "My mom's cool, Ned, but there are two things she never jokes about—Time Surfer missions and being late for supper. Better strap in."

Suzi nodded. "Don't worry, world. Help is on the way!" She turned to the control panel on her right. "Hitting afterburners and setting course for hyperwarp Z22-DH4-B188. Here we go!"

Whoom!

Ned braced himself as the surfie twisted once and shot upward into the sky. Seconds later they were high over the planet, zooming out to the darkness of deep space. The surfie blasted faster and faster. Stars blurred against the darkness.

Roop scanned the black sky. "Entering Omega Sector, Ned. If space is a ball field and Earth is home plate, Omega is definitely the outfield."

"My dad's on a mission out here somewhere," said Suzi. Then she grabbed Ned's arm. "Look!"

Directly in front of them, emerging from the darkness of space, was a giant metal globe, its tubes and spokes all connected to a center shaft.

"Centaur One!" said Roop. "Thirty years ago it was a megadeadly battle station with thousands of people living in it. It was bagel to the max! Now it's a ghost station. Deserted."

"Don't be too sure," cautioned Suzi.

"Right," said Ned. "Don't forget about the signal."

"May I suggest orbiting procedure?" Buzzy put in.

Suzi nodded. "Engage orbiting engines!" She turned to Ned. "We'll surf an orbit of Centaur first, just to be safe."

The surfie veered downward, entering a slow orbit around the huge station.

"We'll also run a scan for life on board," said Roop. "I mean, this was once a pretty nasty tech station, and lots of bad—"

Ka-fwang! A long green beam suddenly shot out from Centaur One and locked on the tiny surfie. It pulled the ship violently toward the station.

Green light flooded the surfie's cabin.

"What's going on?" Ned clung to his seat as the ship pitched left and dived toward the huge station.

"Whoa!" cried Roop. "This orbit's not going too well!"

"Engage thrusters!" shouted Suzi.

Roop jammed down the speed controls. "No go, Sooz! The green beam—it's sucking us down!"

"Excuse me, I have detected a time wave disturbance," crackled Buzzy.

"Wipeout!" yelled Suzi.

Zzngh! All the lights in the surfie went dark.

The green beam pulled the surfie toward a dark circle on the bottom of the station's hull.

"It's like we're magnetized!" yelled Roop.

"No!" Ned cried. "It's like we're—we're—"

CHAPTER 4

"BAGELIZED!"

The surfie lunged out of control toward Centaur One. The green beam pulled it closer, closer, closer . . .

"We're going to crash!" cried Suzi.

"Can't stop it!" Roop grunted over the controls.

Then, just seconds from impact—*vrrrr!* The dark circle on the station's hull spiraled open, and the surfie was sucked inside.

Whoosh! It swooped into an enormous, brightly lit hangar and skidded to a stop on a long landing platform. The engines died.

Suddenly everything was silent.

"What, no welcoming committee?" said Roop with a snort.

"Something's wrong," whispered Suzi.

Ka-chung! The black circle spiraled shut behind them. The sound echoed through the huge empty room.

Roop made a face. "Okay, be that way."

"Well, *someone* must be here," said Ned, gazing out at the huge landing bay around them. "Besides us, I mean."

"And someone," added Roop, "sent that message, remember?"

"Or some*thing*," said Ned worriedly.

Click-click-click. Suzi tried all the surfie's controls. "The power chip's dead. We're stuck here until we juice up. No communicator, no Buzzy, no nothing. I wish my dad was here. He's flying somewhere in the Omega Sector." She sighed. "Boy, are we bageled."

"With cream cheese," mumbled Ned.

"The things you say!" said Roop, climbing out onto the landing platform. "Hmmm. Surfie's dead? Creepy ghost station? Millions of miles from home? But hey, on the bright side . . . on the bright side . . ." He looked around the enormous bay. "Um . . . Suzi, you tell Ned about the bright side. I'm going to check out where we are. Be back in a nanosec."

Roop trotted down a set of stairs to the floor of the landing bay and disappeared through a hatch at the far end.

Ned made a face. "Suzi, what's going on here? I thought this place was deserted."

Suzi stepped from the surfie and surveyed the room. "It's supposed to be. After the shadow wars, tech stations like this were abandoned."

Huge colored pipes rose from the floor to the high ceiling. There were shadowy alcoves on the sides of the room.

"That's what doesn't make sense," she added, walking down the stairs to the bay floor.

"Maybe it's, uh, aliens?" Ned followed Suzi to the center of the huge room.

Roop came running back. "This place is weird. Every light in the whole place is on.

Everything works. It's like someone's home. But who's here? I don't like it."

"I don't like it either," said Suzi, shaking her head slowly.

Ned looked from one to the other. "You don't like it, and you don't like it? Then I *sure* don't like it! This is future stuff, remember? You guys are supposed to know what's going on."

Roop grinned. "Yeah, well, we can all find out together by going through that door." He pointed to a gray hatch in the wall. "Through there is a corridor running straight to the core of Centaur One."

Suzi nodded and started for the hatch. "The core is where we'll find the control center. Find the control center, and we find the answers."

"Oh, man! I don't even know what the questions are!" said Ned, following her.

One by one they slipped through the hatch. They found themselves at the end of a long, high corridor.

"This place is right out of a Zontar comic,"

Ned said. He tapped his back pockets. Zontar cards on one side, personal communicator on the other. Good. He was all set.

The three kids started down the corridor, their steps echoing eerily from one end to the other.

I don't like this, thought Ned. *It's too much like when Mr. Smott surprises you in class. He's so quiet, you don't even know he's there. Then suddenly you look up and bump into his nose! Creepy.*

"I love this!" whispered Roop. "Time Surfers on a mission! Kids doing everything! Kids in total and absolute control!"

"Control?" Ned whispered back. "Not me. You should have seen me in class. I really blew it."

"Again?" Roop said, glancing up at the huge clusters of cabling running along the walls. "Boy, you've got some kind of record for bad things happening in school. You need a vacation."

"No kidding," said Ned. "And if I ever get back, I'll be able to start one."

"Don't worry, we'll get you back."

"Right. At the exact time and place I left. No prob—"

Eeeee.

Ned stopped and squinted at the ceiling. A small silver ball was moving slowly along the high gridwork, flickering. It looked as if it was following them. "Guys? I think we have some company."

Suzi looked up. "An orb robot!"

"Otherwise known as an orbot," said Roop. "A bloog with an attitude!"

"So that's a bloogball?" asked Ned.

"No way. Bloogs are cool," said Suzi. "And they have these things that—"

Ka-zap-zap-zap!

The silver ball blasted a series of thin red beams that exploded down the corridor. Smoke filled the shadows.

Ned froze in his tracks. He watched as a dark shape moved in the smoke. He couldn't see it clearly.

Ka-zap-zap! More blasts. More smoke.

More shapes moving around the smoky shadows.

Ned squinted. He blinked. Then it hit him. Hard. "Pee-yew! What is that horrible sm-sm-sm—"

That was as far as he got.

KLONK! KLONK! HISS!

He saw them, coming out of the shadows at the end of the corridor.

Them.

Bumpy-faced aliens with metal feet and slimy breathing tubes dangling from their heads and back over their shoulders.

"The Klenn!" squeaked Ned, looking at Roop and Suzi. "Um . . . does anybody else think this is weird?"

The green creatures had long, jagged swords and three tongues each.

"Because . . . ," gasped Ned.

The tongues flicked in and out of purple lips.

". . . *I* sure think it's weird!"

The bumpy aliens raised their swords, leaned forward, and charged.

CHAPTER
5

"The evil Klenn!" screamed Ned. "The green, bumpy-faced alien attack army!"

Roop grabbed Ned by the arm. "You *know* these guys?"

"Yes, I know these guys! They're from the Zontar comics. They're terrible! They're nasty! They're baaad dudes!"

KLONK! KLONK! went their metal boots.

HISSSSSSS! went their breathing tubes.

"Whoa! Smells like overzapped fripples!" cried Roop, pinching his nose.

"Huh?" said Ned.

"Stinky!"

"But they can't be real!" yelled Suzi, moving back down the hall.

HISSSSS! More steam rose from the tubes.

"They sure smell real!" Roop shot a look at Ned. "Buddy, you've been hanging with the wrong crowd!"

But that wasn't the worst part.

The worst part was—

Ka-zap!

Ka-zap!

Ka-zap!

That little silver orbot was spitting red beams, and every time a beam exploded on the floor, another bumpy-faced, slime-nosed Klenn warrior rose up from the smoke and joined the others. In minutes there was a whole army of klonking and hissing stinky Klenn.

"Ray guns!" snapped Ned, stepping back up the hall.

"What?" Roop looked at Ned, then at Suzi.

"Ray guns!" Ned repeated. "You know, *zap-zap!* To fight the aliens! Don't you guys have ray guns in your utility belts?"

"No," said Roop. "They're too dangerous."

Ned backed up, holding his nose. "Dangerous? *This* is dangerous!"

KLONK! KLONK! HISS!

KLONK! KLONK! HISS!

The Klenn charged down the corridor after them.

Roop turned to Suzi. "Time to run?"

"Absolutely! Speed shoes!" she screamed, flicking a tiny switch on each of her blinking sneakers. Roop did the same.

Instantly—*rrrr!*—little red flames spewed out from the shoes. Roop and Suzi scooped Ned up by his arms and shot off down the corridor.

KLONK! KLONK! The hall filled with the echoing sound of iron boots thundering on the floor.

The kids raced faster.

"Stop!" yelled Suzi.

"Stop?" Roop screeched. "Those dudes want kids-on-a-stick! They're not going to stop!"

"Not them—us!" she cried. "There's a

hatchway here!" Suzi threw her right hand out and grabbed a pipe hard. The three kids whirled straight into the wall.

Umph! They tumbled through the hatchway into a small room. Suzi jumped back to shut the hatch. It locked tight.

Ned looked around. The room was filled with colored cables, power clusters, and thick wiring. On the ceiling was a small grill-like opening that was blowing warm air down on them.

"Cool move, Sooz," said Roop, rubbing his nose. "Except for the damage to my face."

"Sorry," she said. "It's all I could come up with on such short notice."

KLONK! KLONK! KLONK!

They could hear the Klenn approaching the hatch. Closer. Closer.

Then, nothing. No sound.

Suzi held a finger to her lips.

It was quiet. Very quiet.

Ned took a breath and whispered, "You know, these guys are from a comic book. They aren't even real. How could comic-book aliens come to life? It's crazy. It's impossible. It can't be happening! We must be imagining it!"

Ka-jang! A jagged sword pierced the door and came to a stop one inch from the tip of Ned's nose.

CHAPTER 6

"But hey, I could be wrong about that!"

Plong! Kling! More jagged swords cut holes in the hatch door. Sparks flew everywhere.

Ned grabbed his friends and pulled them to the back of the room. "Let's get out of here!"

Roop watched the swords slicing through the door. "Good idea, Neddo. You first!"

Flang! Another blade pierced the door.

"Okay, okay," said Ned. "I get the point!" He looked at the cables and wiring going up the walls. "First of all, we need a plan."

"No, Ned," said Suzi, dodging another sword. "We need a door!"

"Just what I had in mind," Ned said.

Roop jumped as a sword jammed through the hatchway. "The only door I see is taken!"

Ned pointed to the ceiling. "I think there's some kind of vent up there."

Roop squinted at the ceiling. Then he grinned. "Last one up is human salad!"

Fwip! Fwip! Fwip! In a flash the kids scaled the walls, climbing up the long cables to the top of the room.

Suzi reached out to touch the small opening. "This must be part of the ventilation system," she said.

Ned grabbed the grill and yanked it off. It tumbled to the floor with a bang. He pulled himself through the opening and helped first Suzi and then Roop to climb up, just as—*ga-bong!*—the Klenn broke through the door below and entered the room.

"Ha-ha! Too late!" Roop yelled down at them as he slipped up through the ceiling.

Ned stuck his head up into another corri-

dor. He sniffed for signs of more Klenn. "Smells okay. The air is clear."

"Good thing," said Suzi. "My nose couldn't stand much more of them."

Roop nudged Ned. "Glad you found a quick exit, Neddo. You're pretty good in a tight spot!" He trotted a little way down the long corridor.

Ned smiled. "Thanks."

Suzi looked both ways along the corridor. "That still doesn't explain what's going on here." She turned to Ned. "You said you know all about these guys?"

Ned nodded. "They're the evil Klenn. Really gross aliens from the Zontar comic-book universe. Here, I'll show you."

He dug into his back pocket and flipped through his stack of Zontar trading cards.

"Wait a minute." Ned stopped and flipped through them again.

"It's not here!" he cried in astonishment as he held the cards up for Suzi to see. "I had it! It was here! A card with a foil-embossed 3-D hologram of the evil Klenn. Now it's gone!"

"Wait a second," whispered Suzi, almost to herself. She closed her eyes. "A hologram . . ."

"Of a Klenn soldier," said Ned.

"This is crazy!" said Suzi. "That orbot zaps a couple of red beams into the corridor, and suddenly there's an army of smelly aliens!"

It didn't make sense to Ned, either. How could it happen? How did the Klenn come to life? How did they get to the future? Who brought them here? And what about his missing card?

Roop came running back along the hall. "Look what I found." He held up a black square the size of a postage stamp.

"A power chip," said Suzi. "Now you can fix the surfie!"

Roop frowned and held out his other hand. "But look what else I found." He was holding a little silver box with cables dangling out. "Somebody's been messing around with the hardware. This little box is a subunit wave meter. It's all bageled up."

Ned was still staring at the cards in his

hand. His brain was going a mile a minute. "What if somebody figured out how to make pictures come alive? Like from a comic book. Or a card. Make some kind of—"

Suzi and Roop froze. Ned could see them frowning at each other. *Uh-oh*, he thought. *This isn't good. Not at all.*

"Did I, uh, say something wrong?" Ned asked.

Suzi spoke first. Slowly. A single word. "Vorg."

Roop flinched when she said it. "No way, not Vorg."

Ned stuffed the cards back into his pocket. "Did you say Vorg? You told me once about somebody called Vorg who lives in the Zonk Zone. Is that the Vorg you're talking about?"

Roop nodded. "It's a long story, Neddo. And it's pretty strange."

"We don't know all of it, either," Suzi whispered. "But we think it all started in the first years of the twenty-first century. There was a scientist who called himself Vorg."

"Such a weird name," mumbled Ned.

"He said he'd invented a time travel machine."

"He called it the *Wedge*," added Roop.

Suzi nodded. "He said he would control history with it, going through time and changing things. It would be disastrous. But nobody believed that it would ever work."

"Right," said Roop. "Then he disappeared. I mean, he just vanished. The *Wedge* was never found. Everybody thought he died."

Suzi took a breath. "Until about fifty years later, when a special experimental time computer vanished from a lab station on Mars. And a few years after that, a satellite and a laser telescope disappeared from different parts of the galaxy. Then the shadow wars began."

"Scientists got together and went over all the reports. All the disappearances pointed to Vorg. He was stealing megaspecial gadgets from different time periods."

"To finish the *Wedge*?" Ned asked.

Suzi nodded. "And control time."

Roop shook his head slowly. "And let's face it, Neddo, if someone starts messing around in time with a bad attitude, we're all in megatrouble."

Ned thought about that. He wondered what it meant to mess with time. Could Vorg change history?

"But maybe Vorg is dead?"

Suzi shook her head. "I don't think so. What you said about your missing card . . . Vorg could create armies out of almost nothing. The stories tell about horrible creatures."

"Deadly," said Roop, "just like those stinkheads downstairs. They're called holodroids!"

Ned slumped his shoulders. "Too weird."

"Too weird," Roop repeated. "But true."

Suzi scanned the corridor. "Guys, if Vorg is here, we have to stop him. Kids got rid of wars. We can't let Vorg start them up again. There's no one else but us."

"Kids rule?" asked Ned.

"Kids rule!" said Roop.

Suddenly—*ka-zap-zap-zap!*

"Or maybe not?" asked Ned.

"They're baaaaack!" Roop shouted.

KLONK! KLONK! went the iron feet.

HISSSSSSS! went the floppy breathing tubes.

"They're back, all right," yelled Suzi, "and they're still gross!"

An instant later an army of Klenn came storming from the shadows at the far end of the corridor.

Roop grabbed Ned and Suzi. "Time to blast!"

The kids tore down the corridor, rounded a corner, and stopped dead. Ahead of them was an open door. But it was sliding down fast.

"Too late!" cried Ned, looking back at the advancing Klenn.

"No!" gasped Suzi. "We've got to! It's the control room!"

Ned whirled around.

KLONK! The Klenn were right behind them!

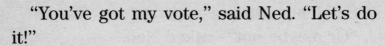

"You've got my vote," said Ned. "Let's do it!"

"Run, drop, and slide!" yelled Roop.

They ran. They dropped. They slid.

They crashed.

Ned got thrown out front and slid under the door just as it came down. *Ka-thung!*

Umph! Umph! Ned heard Roop and Suzi hit the door on the other side as he went sliding across the floor.

He heard klonking and hissing.

Then, nothing.

CHAPTER
7

Cruuuuuunch!

Ned skidded across the control room floor and came to a stop against the far wall.

"Suzi!" he yelled, scrambling back to the door. "Roop!"

No answer. A jab of fear went through him as he thought about his friends.

His friends! In the hands of those ugly, deadly aliens, the evil Klenn!

Ned put his ear to the cold door. All he heard was the rushing of the blood in his own veins.

He was afraid. He was angry. "You better not hurt them!" he cried, banging his fist on the huge metal door. But still he heard nothing from the other side.

"The future," he said, his voice shaking. "I hate it!"

He stood up. *I've got to get help*, he thought. *No use banging on doors. I've got to think.*

Ned stood in a pool of strange green-and-yellow light and looked around. It was a vast circular room, and he was alone in it.

But what a room it was!

It seemed to go on forever. Huge blinking computers, each one larger than the last, lined the room. Weird coiling tubes arched up from the floor to the ceiling fifty feet above.

And towering over everything else was a silver column rising from the center of the floor to an emerald dome at the top.

"The green beam!" Ned gasped. "That must be what sucked us in here!"

Ned scanned his brain to remember everything that had happened so far. *Okay*, he thought. *First we crash-land on a deserted space station. But it's not really deserted. Instead of people, it has holodroids who try to kill us. It's like a comic book. Except that it's real. And my friends are in danger!*

"I can't do this alone," he said. "I've got to get help." He reached around to his back pocket and yanked out his little black communicator. The antenna fell off in his hand.

"No!" Ned cried, squeezing the communicator tightly. But it was definitely broken.

Ned glanced wildly around. He stepped over to a control deck. An electrical panel was torn open, and switches and cables were scattered all about.

Someone had been there! Vorg?

In the center of the mess was a shiny gold cone about eleven inches tall. Sticking up slightly from the top was a black rod, about the thickness of a coat hanger, wound up in a tight coil. At the top was a shiny blue ball.

Ned touched the ball. *Zzzzz!* The rod rose up from the cone and began to twirl. He pulled up on the rod, and it slipped out in his hand.

"Whoa!" Then he stopped. "Wait. I wonder . . ."

He carefully slid the rod into the antenna hole of his communicator. Right away the rod began to twirl and the communicator started to beep.

Diddle-iddle-eep! Diddle-iddle-eep!

Ned laughed. "All right! That's more like it." Carefully adjusting the dials, Ned put the communicator up to his lips. "TS One to Spider Base. This is Ned Banks. I hope you can read me. We're under attack on Centaur One! An evil army of—"

KLUMP-KLUNG!

Something sprang from the shadows on the far side of the room and landed in the light.

Ned whirled around. He nearly fainted. A creature!

It was shaped like a person. Sort of.

It had the arm and leg of a man.

But the rest of it!

The figure groaned and rippled all over, part rubber, part hard metal. The head was bald except for three gleaming bolts sticking out from the forehead. The head pulsed with light.

"Vorg!" Ned gasped.

Sssssss! Steam spurted from Vorg's neck.

"You!" the thing growled back at Ned. Its voice was deep and distant, as if it came from a tunnel.

"M-M-Me?" Ned backed up.

But in a single leap—*KLUNG!*—the creature sprang to the control panel right next to Ned. Vorg leaned forward menacingly. His motions were jerky, as if he was part robot.

Vorg's head twisted nearly all the way around. A shiny black visor stretched from ear to ear.

The steaming rubber-and-metal thing lifted a shiny claw hand and grabbed Ned tightly by the neck. "I am Vorg," he said, "and you are—"

"N-N-Ned," squeaked Ned.

"You are in my *way*!"

The creature's voice was like gravel rolling

in a metal barrel. Ned trembled in fear. He couldn't move.

All at once Vorg let him go. He turned to the control deck and grabbed the golden cone. "This is mine!" He said nothing more. In English, that is.

"Tong! Pra-cho fenn!"

Vrrrr! A silver door shot up on the far side of the room. And in stepped two enormous, smelly Klenn soldiers. In their stinky claws were—

"Roop! Suzi!"

"We're okay!" called Suzi. "So far." She struggled to get free, but the Klenn held her tight.

Ned stepped forward. "We're Time Surfers!" he yelled. "Let them go!"

"And make it quick!" cried Roop. "Before the smell kills us!"

Vorg hissed, a cloud of steam shooting from his neck into the room. "My ugly friends here need someone to play with!"

"But what if we don't want to play with them?" Roop snarled.

"Then you'll play with this!" Vorg waved a claw. *Zap!* A silver ball whizzed down from out of nowhere and settled just over Roop's head.

"Another orbot," snapped Roop. "Too bad I don't have my powerbat."

Silence descended on the room. Thick, heavy silence. Ned felt as if his ears had been instantly stuffed with cotton. It was the strangest feeling. He looked around. What was happening?

Then he saw it. Where there had been nothing before, a large black metal vehicle thundered into view. It looked like a cross between a flying saucer, an army tank, and a massive ax blade.

"The *Wedge*!" gasped Ned.

A second later a ramp lowered from the *Wedge*, and Vorg sprang over to it. Just before hestepped on, he turned to the Klenn.

"*Steng-o hodd!*" he commanded them as the ramp was pulled in.

"Uh-oh," gulped Ned.

Silence fell over the room. The *Wedge* quivered, went hazy, and vanished.

"What did Vorg say to these guys?" Suzi asked.

"It sounded like *stinko-head* to me," said Roop.

The green aliens drew their jagged swords.

"It's Klenn talk," said Ned. "It means 'Kill everyone!' "

Roop made a face. "Oh. In that case, we'd better blast!"

But the orbot blasted first.

CHAPTER 8

Ka-zap-zap-zap!

Red beams shot from the silver orbot and blasted the floor at Ned's feet. Another spray of beams went whistling past his ears.

And just like before, with each new blast another Klenn warrior appeared before the Time Surfers. And each new Klenn began to threaten the kids with its jagged sword.

"I don't like this!" cried Roop, grabbing Ned's arm and pulling him back. "We're getting way outnumbered."

Suzi whirled around, trying to find somewhere to run. "Except that I don't think we actually want to fight these guys!"

Ka-zap!

Ned jumped back from a smoking black hole a half inch from his right sneaker. A Klenn soldier was boiling up out of it.

"We're ` history!" screamed Ned as he scrambled behind a bank of computers.

It looked bad. If they didn't stop that silver ball, in no time they'd have a roomful of aliens with jagged swords that looked like ugly can openers.

"I say we run!" said Suzi.

"I like it!" cried Roop.

In a flash the kids were in motion.

Ka-zap-zap-zap! Before they knew it, there were Klenn everywhere. One with really long breathing tubes pointed at Roop as he stumbled over a computer cable. *"Steng-o chok. Hee!"*

"Oh, it's not that funny!" snapped Roop, diving under the control deck in the center of the room.

But it wasn't a joke. As soon as the Klenn had said that, they split up into two groups

of three and stormed across the room at Roop and Suzi.

"No fair!" yelped Suzi. "Three against one!" Then, without warning, she faked right, cut left, whirled once, and raced across the room to the door.

The Klenn charged after her, one of them grabbing her arm in its claw.

"Let me go!" she cried, tumbling to the ground.

"Soooooozeeee!" shouted Roop, leaping across the open floor toward her.

But the Klenn were waiting for him. Roop managed to dodge two of them, but one really ugly one jumped him from behind and knocked him down.

"Roop!" Ned froze as he saw all six Klenn push his friends into a corner and hold them there.

The orbot hovered above Ned, sizzling and sputtering, waiting for him to make a move.

Ned stepped forward.

Ka-zap-zap! Two new Klenn appeared. In unison they turned to face Ned and started toward him, their swords drawn. There was nowhere to run. He was pinned against the wall.

"Oh, man!" Ned shouted. "Where is Zontar when you need him?" Then it hit him. Zontar! He always said that not only were the Klenn smelly, they were stupid and easy to confuse.

Okay, thought Ned. *Then it just might work.*

And if it didn't? Well, never mind about that.

Ned thrust his hand deep into his back pocket. *Yes*. There they were. The cards. His Zontar cards.

The bumpy aliens approached him slowly, waving their swords in the air.

"*Senk-da-fidd!*" commanded one Klenn.

The silver ball hovered and sputtered overhead, waiting to zap another warrior to life.

Ned glanced at Roop and Suzi. He nodded slowly at each of them.

"Careful, Neddo," Roop whispered.

Then, at just the right moment, when the Klenn were closing in for the kill—

F-f-f-f-f-t-t-t-t-t-t-t-t-t!

The Zontar cards exploded from Ned's hands in an enormous fanlike spray, and the whole room twinkled with rainbow colors.

The Klenn lowered their swords and looked all around. *Yes!* They *were* easy to confuse!

Ka-zap-zap-zaaaap!

The orbot began blasting the cards as they flew toward the ceiling. It tried to shoot down every single card.

Then it happened.

A red laser blast hit one of the cards. But it wasn't just any card. It was the foil-embossed 3-D hologram card with Zontar on it.

The card sizzled as it twirled and fluttered to the ground.

Suddenly a mighty shape appeared before the kids. It was larger than life. It was huge!

Fwank! Fwank! Fwank!

Armor plates sizzled into view, rippling

into place up and down the creature's massive arms and legs. Slung at its sides were twin double-barreled ray guns. And sleek silver wings on each blue boot matched the long fins jutting back from its shoulders. The whole huge shape glittered in the greenish light.

"Whoa!" cried Ned. "It's him!"

"Him who?" asked Roop.

"Him—*Zontar!*"

In a flash, all the Klenn warriors in the room klonked over with their jagged swords and began to chop at Zontar's back.

But the comic-book superhero stood there as if he didn't even feel it. "Yep, kids, it's me, Zontar. I'm a Klenn-buster from way back! And, speaking of *back* . . ."

Zontar swung his massive silver head around and growled at the Klenn attacking him. "That feels good, boys! A little to the left, okay?"

"It *is* Zontar!" cried Ned.

A big, broad grin flashed over the massive

superhero's face. "Ha-ha! The Klenn! I'd keep 'em as pets if they didn't stink so much!"

He gritted his teeth in his huge square jaw and hurled around with a fist the size of a watermelon.

KER-WHUMP!

The Klenn went down like timber! All ten of them fell into a neat stack against the far wall of the control room.

"All right!" yelped Roop. "I like this guy!"

"Ha-ha!" laughed Zontar. "What's not to like?"

Ka-zap-zap-zap! The silver ball made another bunch of very big, very bumpy stink-heads.

"Awww!" cried Zontar. "Their baby brothers wanna play, too!"

WUMP! BOOM!

Another earthshaking blow, and the pile of Klenn nearly reached the ceiling.

Before the silver sphere could zap any more Klenn to life, Zontar whipped out his double-barreled ray guns and blasted the orbot out of the air.

Ka-pow! Pow! Pow!

"Yahoo!" yelled Zontar as the orbot crashed to the floor, fizzling and hissing.

As Ned watched in astonishment, Zontar turned to face him. "Call me next time you're having a Klenn-bashing party," he said, grinning. "Pee-yew! The smell you love to hate!"

He gave a big wave, went hazy, and disappeared as the orbot fizzled its last fizz. Everything grew quiet.

"It was really him!" gasped Ned. "Ernie will go nuts!"

Roop and Suzi ran over to Ned and nearly crushed him in a bear hug. "Zommo!" said Roop. "You are one incredible dude!"

Ned laughed as he started for the corridor. "Hey, we're official Time Surfers. This is the kind of stuff we do!"

Five minutes later, the kids were in the landing bay. Roop had just finished putting the new power chip into the surfie's control panel.

Va-room! The little purple ship lifted into

the air and banked off the platform toward the bay doors. *Vrrrr!* They spiraled open.

But there, where there should have been empty space, was a giant silver spaceship, coming in fast. Huge iron jaws were opening on the front.

The surfie was going to be swallowed up!

"Uh-oh!" yelled Suzi.

"Zommo!" cried Roop.

"More aliens?" shouted Ned.

CHAPTER 9

Klang! The giant jaws closed around the purple surfie.

Trapped! Inside another spaceship!

An instant later a strange-looking figure stepped out on a platform above them.

"A bug man with purple eyes!" cried Ned. "Hide!"

But Suzi didn't hide. She jumped from the surfie, ran up to the creature, and hugged it. "This is no bug man," she said, her face beaming. "This is my dad!"

The creature took off its purple helmet. There was a face under it. It was smiling.

Roop patted Ned on the back. "Aliens, huh?"

"I was just joking," said Ned sheepishly. "I knew it was her dad. Really."

Commander Naguchi gave a snap wave to Roop and introduced himself to Ned. "I heard your distress signal from the other side of the Omega Sector, Ned. We came as fast as we could. Are you all right?"

"We're fine," said Suzi, smiling. "And thanks to Ned, we got some special help." She winked at Ned.

"Big help!" said Roop. "Silver, with lots of jokes."

Suzi nodded. "The bad news is that Vorg's back."

Commander Naguchi's expression turned serious. "We'd better go straight to Spider Base and make a report."

"Blast-o, fast-o, Suzi," said Ned. "And after Spider Base, I'd better get back home. I've got a game to finish and a vacation to start!"

"No prob," said Roop. "We'll go into hyper-warp just for you!"

A few minutes later, Ned was gazing back into the darkness of space as the surfie blasted away from Centaur One.

He watched his two friends working the controls for a while. Then he took his communicator from his back pocket and pulled out the new antenna that stuck out of the top, the antenna that came from the control room. It twirled around and around.

"I wonder what that golden cone thing was that Vorg took from Centaur," Ned said. "I mean, what if he really starts changing time?"

Roop turned to Ned. "Then we'll change *his* time. I'll give him some major *time out*! He'll do some *time*! We'll bagel him *big-time*! There's no *time* like—"

Suzi shot Ned a look and shook her head. "Thanks, Ned."

"For what?"

"If it wasn't for you, I'd have to sit through Roop's jokes all by myself!"

"Hey!" cried Roop, pretending to be hurt,

but smiling. "It takes me a long *time* to think of jokes like these!" He chuckled to himself.

The stars stretched and blurred all around the ship; then—*voom!*—they shot behind a big green moon and swirled down a shimmering tunnel of blue and silver.

The blue and silver of a timehole.

Suzi turned around. "Next stop, Lakewood School, baseball field, ninth inning . . ."

Ned settled back in his seat. He was going home.

CHAPTER 10

Smack!

When Ned's feet hit the ground, he was back on the baseball field at Lakewood School, running deep into center field.

Above him, a cloud of dust and a purple flash swooped through the air. Roop and Suzi smiled down from the surfie's dome. After a couple of quick snap waves, his friends were gone, through the dust cloud and straight up into a timehole. Gone. To the future!

Okay, Ned told himself. *Back to reality.* He took a quick look around. Everything looked normal.

Good, he thought. The exact place and time he'd left the game. He probably hadn't even been missed. At least he hoped so.

You had to be careful coming back into time. If you came back at the wrong moment, it could get pretty weird. And that day had been weird enough.

Ned needed a break. A vacation.

Yes! Vacation! It was Friday afternoon. Ernie should be coming any minute. What could be better?

Ned took a quick look in his glove. The ball was there. *Excellent! Okay, I can stop running now. I'll just wait for the dust to clear, hold up the ball, and wait for the standing ovation. The cheers! The screams from the crowd!*

"Baaaanks!" Coach Fensterman screamed. "The ball! *Catch the ball!*"

"Huh?" Ned looked in his glove. "But I've already got the ball!"

Kkkkkkrrrkkkkk!

The air crackled like lightning.

"Wha—?" Something was wrong.

Then he saw it. A baseball flying toward him. High and fast.

Oh, no! He hadn't come back at the exact time he'd left. He must have come back just *before*. The problem was, he'd come back with the ball. And here was that ball again!

Kkkkk! The air rippled with energy as the second ball approached.

Ned instantly remembered the first law of time travel. When two of the same thing are in the same place at the same time—watch out! Energy explosion! Zonk Zone time!

Or, as Roop would say it, baseball plus baseball equals *KA-BOOM!*

"I've got to get rid of this ball!"

The dust cloud completely surrounded him. There was only one thing to do. Ned snatched the first ball from his glove and shot it behind him. It disappeared into the tall grass behind the outfield.

"The ball! Catch the ball!"

Ned whirled around in the dust.

He raised his arm. He searched the sky

just as the dust was clearing. He opened his glove.

Smack!

The baseball struck the side of his glove, dribbled down his arm, and fell to the ground.

The dust cleared enough for Ned to see the runner scoring. He also saw Coach Fensterman down on all fours, chewing on his cap and pounding the grass with his fists.

Ned lost the game.

That's how everyone would remember him. The kid who was looking the wrong way when the baseball hit his glove.

The game was over, and everybody swarmed onto the field. Ned just stood there, watching the dust swirling past him.

One more second. One more second and he would have been remembered as the kid who *caught* the ball. He would have been a hero.

Ned looked up. The hazy cloud was drifting away across the baseball field. Here and

there the dust swirled and rose and glittered in the afternoon sun like a galaxy of tiny stars.

Beep! Beep!

Ned reached for his communicator, but it wasn't on.

He saw a car pulling into the school parking lot on the far side of the field. A kid got out and started running toward him.

"Ernie!" Ned dashed over. When they met in left field, it was like an energy explosion. They jumped up and down and kicked up their own huge cloud of dust.

"It's incredible to see you!" Ned said.

"You too!"

Suddenly everything seemed better to Ned. Things would be getting back to normal now.

Snacking in front of the TV. Shooting hoops on the playground. Normal stuff.

Ned's mother walked over to them. "I'm so glad you two will be spending some time together."

"Yeah," said Ned with a laugh. "Lots of time."

As they walked to the car Ned caught a glimpse of Mr. Smott running from the school, yelling something. He stopped when he saw Ned, stared back at the school, then back at Ned.

"Uh-oh," muttered Ned. "Does he know?" He trembled at the thought. Did Mr. Smott know about him and time? And him and the future?

"Whoa!" said Ernie, watching Mr. Smott beginning to frown. "Donut!"

"Excuse me?" said Ned's mother.

"He means *bagel*, Mom. But there's no time to explain. Hit the afterburners and go into hyperwarp. Let's blast!"

"Uh . . . okay," she said, starting up the car.

Ernie jumped in next to Ned. "I almost forgot. Take a look at these." He pulled a stack of trading cards from his jacket pocket. "The new series of Zontar cards—*The Battle for*

Time! They're awesome. I got a set for you, too!"

Ned looked down at the shiny cards, then back across the dusty field at Mr. Smott. "Oh no," he said. "Here we go again!"